WITHDRAW

MW00910048

# *Disney Adventures*

## ⑥

# CASEBUSTERS

### Secret of the Time Capsule

# Secret of the Time Capsule

By Joan Lowery Nixon

New York

With love to Andrew Thomas Quinlan—J. L. N.

# 1

I'VE GOT EXCITING news for you fourth graders," Mrs. Jackson said. She looked mysterious. "Soon, you're going to hear from people from the past."

Sean Quinn leaned forward, poking Debbie Jean Parker to be quiet. He knew that Mrs. Jackson wasn't going to say another word until everyone had settled down.

The moment the classroom was silent, Mrs. Jackson asked, "How many of you have ever heard of a time capsule?"

Henry Craft raised his hand. "Does it have something to do with outer space?" he asked.

"No, it doesn't," Debbie Jean interrupted.

"A time capsule is a container that holds a whole bunch of things from a certain time. It's usually buried. Then it's dug up years and years later and opened."

"Why?" Matt Fischer asked.

"So people can see what life was like way back when." Debbie Jean wiggled with self-importance.

"That's right," Mrs. Jackson said. "And right here in Redoaks, in the year 1918, a time capsule was buried. It was supposed to be opened in one hundred years."

"I know, I know, I know!" Debbie Jean shouted. "The mayor's secretary, Emma Wegman, lives next door to us, and she told me all about it, and when it's going to be opened, and there's going to be a parade and a party, and—"

"Thank you, Debbie Jean," Mrs. Jackson said. "Let's talk about how this class is going to be involved. One of the items in the time capsule was an envelope filled with letters from fourth graders. The letters are addressed to the fourth graders of the future."

"If the capsule hasn't been opened, how do we know it's got letters in it?" Matt asked.

Debbie Jean blurted out, "Because Miss Wegman found the list of contents in one of the city hall's files."

Sean did some quick mental arithmetic and said, "Mrs. Jackson, if that time capsule was supposed to be opened in one hundred years, it would be the year 2018, not now."

"That's right, Sean," Mrs. Jackson said, "but something happened to change things. The capsule was buried during a ceremony to celebrate the fifty years that had passed since the founding of Redoaks. It was buried under the bronze statue of John M. Williford. In 1918, he was the mayor of Redoaks."

"I was in the park yesterday," Jabez Amadi said, "and that big old statue was down and lying on the ground."

"The statue had to be taken down," Mrs. Jackson said. "One side of the hill under the statue eroded so much that the statue began to tilt. There was a danger that at any time it could fall. Someone could have been badly hurt . . . or even killed. Soon the statue will be moved to a safer place."

"Why couldn't they just move the time capsule with the statue and save it to be opened in 2018?" Sean asked. "Why open it early?"

"I know! I know why!" Debbie Jean jumped up and down at her desk, waving her hands. "It's because when Miss Wegman found the list of what was inside the capsule, she showed it to the mayor. He decided that the time capsule should be opened right away."

"Maybe it's like getting a birthday present early, and you can't wait to open it," Matt suggested.

"Settle down, now. We're getting to the

really big news," Mrs. Jackson said. "The members of this class, just like the fourth graders of 1918, are going to write letters to the kids who'll be fourth graders one hundred years from now."

"How big is this capsule?" Jennifer Doaks asked. "How much will it hold?"

"I don't have the exact figures on the size," Mrs. Jackson said, "but I understand it's a round, airtight metal tube. It's about two feet in diameter and about three feet long."

Sean looked at the figures he'd been adding and subtracting on a piece of notebook paper. "If those kids were nine in the fourth grade, they would have been born in 1909. But the capsule's going to be opened early, so they won't be 109 years old. Some of them may still live in Redoaks. Why don't we find out and invite them to the party?"

Mrs. Jackson beamed. "What a wonderful idea, Sean!" she said.

Debbie Jean shook her head. "No, it isn't," she said. "No one will know the names of the kids until the capsule is opened, and then it will be too late to invite anybody."

*Bummer!* At first, Sean felt the same sinking feeling in the pit of his stomach that hit him every time Debbie Jean really bugged him. But as the answer to the problem popped into his mind, he laughed. "Schools keep records," he said. "We could find the kids' names that way."

"Good thinking," Mrs. Jackson said. "I'll volunteer to go through the records. Sean, would you like to trace the names, once I get them, and see how many of these former students you can track down?"

"I'll help," Debbie Jean said. "I was thinking of exactly the same idea. Sean just happened to say it first."

Matt slowly raised a hand. "I know someone who was in the fourth grade in 1918. His name's Mr. Boris Vlado, and he lives on our block with his daughter's family. A couple of times he's talked about when he was in school and wrote something for a time capsule. I didn't pay much attention to what he said because . . . uh, because . . ."

"Because why?" Sean finally asked.

Matt's words tumbled out in a rush. "Because Mr. Vlado talks about a lot of strange things. He said there was something danger- ous in that capsule. And he's also said that he's seen UFOs hovering over the bus terminal. And he knows for a fact that aliens hide out in the basement of the city hall."

Sean wanted to laugh until he saw Matt was really afraid.

"I'd just as soon stay away from Mr. Vlado," Matt said. "He's so weird he scares me!"

# 2

THE STORY ABOUT the time capsule was on the front page of the next morning's *Redoaks News*.

John Quinn put down his coffee cup and read aloud, "The ceremony will be held on Saturday, complete with a parade and a band concert in the park."

"There'll be speeches, no doubt," Dianne Quinn said.

"Speeches? Right," Mr. Quinn answered. "City Councilman Victor Williford will give a speech about his grandfather, the late John M. Williford, mayor in 1918. And, of course, our mayor, Harry Harlow, plans to give a speech in honor of the occasion."

"Maybe there'll be a speech in honor of Boris Vlado," Sean added.

Brian reached across the table for another slice of toast. "Who's Boris Vlado?" he asked.

Sean swallowed a long slurp of orange juice, then told his family about the fourth-grade letters and what his class planned to do.

"What a wonderful idea," Mrs. Quinn said. "Sean, we're proud of you for thinking of inviting any former fourth graders who are still living in Redoaks."

"This sounds like a good project for the Casebusters," Mr. Quinn said. "Bring me the list of names, and I'll show you how you can try to trace them by computer search."

"If the women married, they'd have different names than they had at school," Brian said.

"That's right," Mr. Quinn said. "However, if they were married in the Redoaks area, there's a county department that will give you information about marriage certificates."

Mrs. Quinn looked at her watch and pushed back her chair. "I've got to run," she said. "We're right in the middle of a big advertising promotion for one of our main accounts."

"I've got an early meeting, too," Mr. Quinn said. "You boys have exactly twenty minutes until it's time to leave for school. Watch your time. Don't be late."

"We won't," Brian answered.

"Listen to this, Bri!" Sean had spread the front section of the newspaper across the table and was leaning on it. "Here's a list of the stuff that was buried inside the capsule. There's a copy of the local newspaper from November 30, 1918; a copy of *California Pix,* a monthly magazine; and an essay written about the armistice that had been signed at the end of World War I on November 11. And there's a journal with the history of Redoaks written by the members of the Ladies' Lawn Tennis, Sewing Circle, and Historical Society. I bet Mrs. Helen Hemsley was president, even way back then."

Thinking about bossy Mrs. Hemsley, Sean burst out laughing. It took a minute before he could go on. "There's a letter praising Redoaks's citizens written by California's governor in 1918—William D. Stephens—to Mayor Williford. And there are lots of photographs, and the fourth graders' letters, and something from Mayor Williford that just says, 'My gift to the city I love.'"

"What is the gift?" Brian asked.

"It doesn't say."

"The reporter should have asked Councilman Williford. His grandfather probably told him what it was."

Sean put down the newspaper. "There's nothing in the story about anything that could be dangerous," he said.

Brian turned from the sink. "Dangerous? What are you talking about?"

"What Boris Vlado told Matt." Sean went on to recount the conversation he hadn't remembered to tell earlier.

"This Mr. Vlado said there was something dangerous in the capsule?" Brian asked. "I wonder if he was talking about explosives."

"Matt said Mr. Vlado is scary and talks about a lot of weird stuff, like seeing UFOs," Sean said, but he surprised himself by shivering. "Bri, what if there really is something dangerous in that capsule?"

"That's something we'd better find out before it's opened," Brian said.

"How?"

Brian dried his hands on the dish towel and reached for his backpack. "Come on. Get your books. Ask Matt where Boris Vlado lives. After school you and I are going to pay him a visit."

\*     \*     \*

Sean got Mr. Vlado's address from Matt and the list of 1918 fourth graders from Mrs. Jackson.

"Only eight names?" he asked in surprise.

"Redoaks was a very small community at that time," Mrs. Jackson said. "Do you think you can track them down?"

Sean smiled. "One down, seven to go."

Debbie Jean could hardly wait until after roll had been taken to make her announcement.

"My father volunteered to help build one of the floats in the parade," she said. "He promised to let me ride on it as Miss Fourth-Grade Redoaks! I'll wear a gorgeous costume and probably a crown, and wave to everyone in the crowd."

The other girls in the class started oohing and squealing, but Sean mumbled, "Yuck!" and slid down in his seat. Sometimes girls were weird.

Matt leaned across the aisle and said, "Sean, if it's okay with you, Jabez and I won't go with you and Brian to see Mr. Vlado. The guy's too creepy."

"Huh! You're some friends," Sean said.

"We are friends, and if you had to go alone we'd go with you. Honest. But you said Brian will be there, and he's thirteen. He's a lot better protection than we'd be."

"Protection from what?" Cold shivers trickled up and down Sean's backbone.

"I—I didn't say that right, I guess." Matt shook his head. "Mr. Vlado wouldn't do anything to hurt you. He'll just tell you some scary stuff. And he looks scary. His eyes are kind of wild and—"

Mrs. Jackson rapped on her desk. "Come to order, class. I want you to spend some time after school thinking about what you can tell the kids of the future in the letters you'll be writing. Make a list of things we use in our daily lives, from alarm clocks to computers, and bring it to school tomorrow." She opened a math book and added, "Right now, let's see how well you do on a short quiz."

BRIAN AND SEAN rode their bikes over to Matt's street and quickly found the house where Boris Vlado lived. It was set back from the street and surrounded by broad-limbed shade trees, but its mustard gold paint had faded and yellowed in streaks. On each side of the front door was a large pot of geraniums, but none of the plants were blooming. They'd been badly choked out by weeds.

Mr. Vlado answered the door. He had once been a fairly tall man, Brian decided, but now he stood hunched over, scowling up at Sean and Brian from under bushy eyebrows.

"Go away," he said. "I don't talk to salesmen."

"We're not selling anything," Brian quickly explained. "I'm Brian Quinn. This is my brother, Sean. My brother's class at school wants to invite you to a party."

"*Hummph*! I don't go to parties," Mr. Vlado grumbled.

"This is a party for the whole city," Sean explained. "It's going to be next Saturday when the time capsule is opened."

"The time capsule?" For an instant Mr. Vlado's small, dark eyes opened wider, and he chuckled.

"We'd like you to come with the fourth grade to the ceremony in the park," Sean said, "and watch the mayor open the capsule."

Again Mr. Vlado chuckled. "Maybe he'd better not open it," he said.

Brian stepped forward. "Mr. Vlado, we'd like to ask you some questions about the capsule. Is it okay if we come in?"

Mr. Vlado nodded. Then he slowly turned, leaning on his cane, and led the way into the dimly lit living room. All the shades were down, but Brian and Sean could see that the furniture was heavy and squat. The brown plush on the sofa was so old and stiff that it scratched their arms and backs.

Brian pulled out his investigator's notebook and pen. "Why shouldn't the mayor open the time capsule?" he asked.

"I don't know," Mr. Vlado answered.

"But you just told us that maybe he shouldn't open it."

Mr. Vlado chuckled again and rested his chin on the head of his cane. "Maybe no one should open it."

"Why?" Brian asked.

"I don't know."

Brian and Sean looked at each other while Mr. Vlado watched them carefully, his eyes darting back and forth. Mr. Vlado was aware of something, Brian thought. But how was Brian going to get him to tell them what it was?

Brian closed his notebook. "Thank you for

talking to us," he said. "You were only nine years old in 1918. We should have realized that you were too young to know anything important about the contents of the time capsule."

He began to stand, but Mr. Vlado waved his cane at him.

"Sit down and pay attention," he said. "I wasn't too young to *hear* things. I heard my father talking to my mother about when the time capsule would be opened. He said, 'I think they made a bad choice. It could blow up in their faces.'"

Sean gasped, and Brian asked, "Did he think someone had put explosives in the capsule?"

"My father wasn't talking about explosives," Mr. Vlado said. "If he knew about explosives he would have stopped the mayor from burying the capsule. I think he was talking about some kind of information that's inside that capsule. Something that's going to upset somebody."

"What?" Sean asked.

"I told you," Mr. Vlado said, "I don't know."

Brian stood, and Sean scrambled to get up. "Mr. Vlado, we'll send you an invitation to come to the park with our class next Saturday for the ceremonies. We hope you'll change your mind and come."

"Maybe I will," he said. "If something's going to happen, I want to be there to see it."

"Do you know if any of your classmates are still in Redoaks?"

Mr. Vlado struggled to stand. He leaned into Sean's face. "Only four of them," he said, "and you can count on it. They'll be on hand."

"Great!" Sean said. He pulled the list Mrs. Jackson had given him from the pocket of his jeans. He handed it to Mr. Vlado. "Can you tell us their names and where we can find them?"

Mr. Vlado jabbed at the paper with one finger, then shoved it at Sean. "They're long gone from Redoaks except Cropper, Jones,

Murphy, and Slade. And they're all at the same address."

"What is it?" Sean asked.

Mr. Vlado's eyes bored into Sean's, and his words came out in a hiss. "The cemetery," he said.

# 3

ON THE WAY HOME Brian said, "Let's stop off at the park. I'm curious about that time capsule."

Sean pedaled faster to keep up. "There's no way we can see the capsule. Nobody can see what's in it. It's going to stay buried until it's dug up at the opening ceremony."

"Let's make sure," Brian said.

"What are you talking about?" Sean asked.

But Brian had parked his bike and was already walking across the grass toward the small hill on which the statue of John M. Williford had rested.

"Look," Sean said. "It's just like Jabez said.

The statue is down on the ground."

"The marble base under the statue has been moved, too," Brian said. He stared into a large, square hole that was about two feet deep. In the center of the hole the dirt had been brushed away, and he could see the top of a metal container. The rim was sealed shut with red sealing wax.

A sudden shout made both Brian and Sean jump. A tall park employee, dressed in a work uniform, strode toward them. The top of his bald head gleamed pink in the late afternoon sunshine. "Hey, you kids! Get away from there!" he yelled.

"It's okay. We're not touching anything," Sean answered.

"We're Brian and Sean Quinn," Brian said. "We just came to see where the time capsule is buried."

Sean pointed. "Is that it in there?"

"Yes, that's it," the man said. "It's part of my

job to make sure it stays there."

He wore a badge with his name on it: Hugh Dickerson.

Brian memorized the name. He knew that sometimes a private investigator doesn't want people to know that he's investigating. When he can't pull out a notebook and write down important information, he uses his memory and makes notes later.

"You kids run along," Mr. Dickerson said.

"Who took the statue down?" Brian asked.

"My brother Gene and I did," Mr. Dickerson said. "Along with tackle and a pulley and a truck motor to help with the heaviest part."

Brian pointed at the hole in the ground. "I bet it was hard to get that marble base out of there," he said.

"Terrible hard," Mr. Dickerson answered. "And it didn't help to have so many people come rushing over to watch."

"Who were the people?" Brian asked.

"And how did they know about it?" Sean added.

Mr. Dickerson frowned as he thought. "I suppose they knew about it because it was city business," he said. "The mayor and the city council and some other people from city hall were all here."

"Did any of them want to open the capsule?" Brian asked.

"Oh, sure. The mayor did. He said he should be in charge of it. He insisted he should keep it in his office until it was time to bury it again. But that grandson of the old guy who posed for the statue . . ."

"Councilman Victor Williford," Brian said.

"Yeah. Anyhow, he didn't want the time capsule to be opened. He said at least it should stay where it was until they decided what to do with it. Then the mayor's secretary said there ought to be a ceremony and they could open it then. Most of them went along with that."

"I wonder why the mayor didn't post a guard," Brian said.

"He did," Mr. Dickerson insisted. "During the day my brother and I take turns guarding the place. Then at night the police keep an eye on it."

Sean piped up, "Shouldn't a guard be on hand all the time?"

"A guard *is* on hand," Mr. Dickerson said. "You see me here, don't you?"

"You weren't here when we came," Brian said.

Mr. Dickerson turned red, right to the top of his head. "I have to leave once in a while," he mumbled and pointed toward a toolshed in the distance. "And I can't spend all day talking to you," he said grumpily. "G'wan home. Do your homework or something. Stop hanging around here bugging me."

As Sean and Brian walked toward their bikes, Sean said, "How come you asked so many questions about guarding the capsule, Bri?"

"I just want to have all the facts," Brian said. He pulled out his notebook and wrote the names of Hugh and Gene Dickerson. Then he made a note of what Hugh Dickerson had told him.

"You don't think someone will try to steal the capsule, do you?"

"They wouldn't have enough time, if Mr. Dickerson's schedule was right. The capsule's big, and it's heavy."

"Couldn't they take off the top, right where it is?"

"You saw all that dried red wax around the lid of the container. It would have to be chipped off. It would show it had been opened."

Brian pulled his bike from the rack and kicked back the stand. "Do you want to see some of what's in that capsule?" he asked.

Sean nearly fell off his bike. "What are you talking about, Bri? How are we going to see what's in the capsule, if nobody else can?"

Brian grinned. "We can see duplicates. We know the dates of both the newspaper and the copy of *California Pix*. They probably have a copy on microfilm at the library. And the November 30, 1918, issue of the *Redoaks News* will be on file at the newspaper office."

"Why do you want to see them?"

"I'm curious," Brian said. "I want to know why the mayor insisted on opening the capsule before one hundred years were up. Maybe a story in the magazine or newspaper will give us the reason. Come on, Sean. Let's go to the library first."

Brian was right. The November 1918 issue of *California Pix* had been filmed. The librarian threaded the film through the microfilm machine, and Brian and Sean slowly scanned it. It was a thin magazine, so they easily found what they were searching for on page eighteen, close to the end.

"Look. Here's an article about John M. Williford and his large stamp collection. No wonder they put this issue into the time capsule," Brian said.

Brian and Sean leaned forward to read the praise for Mr. Williford's outstanding role as a businessman and for his highly generous contributions to local charities. Two photographs were with the article. One showed Mr. Williford holding a page of rare stamps in his collection. The other showed him—his eyes twinkling with delight—as he held forward a letter that had been sent to him by William D. Stephens, at that time the governor of California.

There was something odd about that picture, Brian thought, but he couldn't put his finger on it. Maybe it was Mr. Williford. He had that same kind of mischievous look Dad got when he talked about being a boy and playing tricks on Halloween.

Sean, who'd been leaning forward studying the article and photograph, sat back. "Weird," he said.

Brian looked at him in surprise. "You saw it, too?"

"Yeah," Sean said.

Brian sighed. "But there was nothing in that article that would embarrass Mr. Williford or his grandson."

"Maybe what we're looking for will be in the newspaper," Sean told him. He looked up at the large clock over the checkout desk. "We've got time to go to the newspaper offices, haven't we?"

"We'll give it a try," Brian said. "But we'd better hurry. We might have to read all the way to the back page, and the newspaper will be a lot longer than this magazine."

Brian was soon surprised to find he was

wrong. The lead headline on page one was: "Indicted for Bank Fraud." The story stated that a Roger Harlow, bank teller, was the culprit who had been indicted. Not only that, but his partner in crime was a fellow bank employee, Amos Wegman!

"Harlow and Wegman!" Sean said. "Bri, our mayor's name is Harry Harlow, and his secretary's name is Emma Wegman! Do you think Roger and Amos were their relatives?"

"It's an easy guess," Brian said. "How many people in Redoaks have the names Harlow and Wegman?"

Sean shook his head. "This must be what Mr. Vlado's father meant when he talked about something that could blow up in their faces. It wasn't very nice of the city officials to put a copy of this newspaper in the time capsule."

"They always put the newspaper printed the day a time capsule is buried," Brian said. "Anyhow, nobody could possibly know way back then that when the capsule was opened Harry Harlow would be our mayor."

"Or that Emma Wegman would be his secretary."

Brian frowned. "I don't understand why Mayor Harlow was so eager to open the capsule. If there was a story like that about somebody I was related to, I'd want it to stay buried."

"Maybe he didn't know."

"Or maybe that's why he wanted to take care of the capsule until it was buried again. He could pull the newspaper out, and no one would know the difference."

"If we're right, Mayor Harlow and Emma Wegman aren't very happy about what's in that capsule," Sean said.

"And they're going to feel even worse when the capsule is opened," Brian added.

They left the library and headed for home, but as they turned their bikes up the driveway Sean said, "I don't get it. Mr. Dickerson told us that Mayor Harlow wanted the capsule to be opened, and Councilman Williford wanted it to be buried again, without opening it. But the newspaper and magazine stuff we found made the Harlows and Wegmans look bad and the Willifords look good. Shouldn't it be the other way around?"

Brian leaned his bike against the fence. He thought about the photograph of Mr. Williford holding up the letter from the governor. What was it about that picture that bothered him? He wished he knew.

As Brian opened the back door, he said, "There's something strange about the whole thing. I don't know how it fits into the case."

John Quinn put down the phone as Brian and Sean came into the kitchen. "I just received a phone call from Emma Wegman," he said. "One of the park employees complained to her that you boys were prowling around the time capsule. You not only didn't leave when he told you to but also pestered him with questions and even accused him of not doing his duty as guard."

"Dad! That's not the way it happened at all," Sean complained.

"Well, in a way it's sort of right, but in another way it isn't," Brian said. "Dad, you know we wouldn't be rude to anybody."

"I know," Mr. Quinn said, "but Miss Wegman was upset."

"Dad . . . ," Sean began.

"Did you find the information you wanted about the 1918 fourth graders?" Mr. Quinn asked.

"Yes," Sean said. "Boris Vlado's the only one."

"Then you've done what you set out to do," Mr. Quinn said. "Let's leave it at that."

"But our case—"

"Come on, Casebusters," Mr. Quinn said. "Face facts. This case is closed."

S EAN WROTE an invitation to Boris Vlado to attend the parade and ceremony with Mrs. Jackson's fourth-grade class. To Sean's surprise, Mr. Vlado's daughter accepted for him.

Mrs. Jackson arranged for Mr. Vlado to ride on the float with Debbie Jean, with the fourth graders marching as a guard of honor on both sides of the float. The theme of the parade would be "Yesterday, Today, and Tomorrow."

All week Sean wished that Saturday would come soon. It wasn't because he was eager for the parade and ceremonies. It was because he couldn't stand hearing Debbie Jean gush on and on about her gorgeous dress, and her beautiful crown, and how she and Mr. Vlado would be photographed by the television and newspaper camera crews.

Debbie Jean's father had fastened twin thrones, where Debbie Jean and Mr. Vlado would be sitting, on a platform on top of the hood of the truck. And he'd built what looked like a space shuttle on the flatbed.

"You should have seen how hard it was to put in place," Debbie Jean said. "That shuttle is awfully heavy. It's going to look fantastic, and I am, too."

Maybe it will rain, Sean hoped. Debbie Jean might melt, just like the witch in *The Wizard of Oz*.

But on the day of the parade the sky was clear and the temperature was perfect. The *Redoaks News* predicted a huge turnout for the parade and ceremony.

Sean couldn't help feeling proud. The fourth graders' float looked great. The miniature space shuttle was covered with strips of crepe paper that rustled in the breeze. Strings of brightly colored banners flew behind it. It rose into the sky almost like the real thing.

Debbie Jean, wearing her Halloween princess costume and a rhinestone crown, climbed into place. She clutched a bouquet of mixed flowers from her mother's garden. Sean was sorry the bouquet didn't have some stinkweed in it.

There were other floats, many of them decked in red, white, and blue. Some of the float riders carried flowers and some wore costumes from the early decades of the twentieth century. There were clowns and horseback riders, and at the head of the parade, in shiny new convertibles, rode Mayor Harry Harlow and the members of the city council.

Most of the fourth graders marched with

Mrs. Jackson, close to the head of the truck, but Sean lagged behind. By the time they had almost reached the park he was walking alone, next to the flatbed. His thoughts were on the time capsule and what Mayor Harlow and his secretary would say when the newspaper was opened.

"Sean!" he heard Brian yell. "Sean! Look out!"

Sean glanced up to see his brother pushing toward him through the edge of the crowd. The people who were looking in Sean's direction froze in terror. Some gasped or screamed. A few started to run toward Sean.

Brian was first. He shoved Sean and shouted, "The shuttle! It's falling! Get out of the way! Run!"

Sean looked up to see that the shuttle's supports had given way. The heavy cone had cracked and was dropping down upon him!

Sean ran, stumbling into Brian. With a loud

whack, the shuttle smashed on the street, right where he'd been standing.

As people screamed and yelled, the parade came to a stop. Officials from the front cars ran back to see what had happened.

"Thank goodness you weren't hurt!" Mrs. Jackson said over and over.

Debbie Jean screeched, "Sean! What did you do to my float?"

Sean leaned against Brian, his knees wobbling. "Bri! The shuttle just missed me!" he cried out. "It would have fallen on me if you hadn't been here."

Some of the men in the crowd dragged the shuttle off to one side. "That's strange," one of them said. "The way this support broke off, it looks almost like it was sawed through."

"Couldn't have been," another said. "Nobody'd do a thing like that."

"It must have been badly designed," someone else suggested. "The cone was probably too heavy for its base."

Mr. Vlado was helped off his perch on the float. He hobbled to where Brian and Sean were standing and shook his head. "They showed up, didn't they?" he said. "In spite of not getting invitations."

"Who?" Brian asked.

"Cropper, Jones, Murphy, and Slade. The ones in the cemetery. You can thank them for spoiling the parade. They didn't like not being invited."

Sean gasped and whispered to Brian, "Ghosts did that?"

"No," Brian said, wishing that Mr. Vlado wasn't quite so creepy. "Don't even think about it. I'm sure that the space shuttle broke because of its own weight. It had to have been an accident."

Most of the crowd had drifted into the park, and the floats were being parked along the street. Brian lingered to run his fingers over the broken support under the shuttle. He gasped. It *had* been deliberately sawed. Somebody had planned for the shuttle to fall.

"Come on, Bri," Sean called. "The mayor's giving his speech."

Brian wanted to talk to Dad, or maybe his friend Detective Thomas Kerry of the police force. But they weren't on hand, so he hurried to catch up with Sean.

Brian had just reached a place at the edge of the crowd, where he could see the row of dignitaries balance on wobbling folding chairs, when his parents showed up.

"Sorry we missed the parade," Mrs. Quinn said. "Your father got a long-distance call he had to take. Have they begun the speeches yet?"

Nearby, a woman nodded and put a finger to her lips.

But Brian couldn't wait. He whispered to his dad, "Did you see the shuttle lying in the street?"

Mr. Quinn looked puzzled, "No. Where in the street?"

"Be right back," Brian said. He dashed to the street, where a city dump truck was just hauling away the broken remains of the shuttle. "Wait!" he yelled at the driver.

The driver leaned down from the open window. "Can't wait," he said. "Orders. Straight from the city council. Big crowd. Gotta clear the street."

The truck rumbled off, and Brian walked back to join his parents. *Whose orders?* he wondered. If the shuttle was hauled off and destroyed, no one would be able to say for sure if the supports had been sawed through or not.

"Is something the matter?" Mr. Quinn asked Brian.

"I had to go see about the shuttle," Brian began.

"*Shhhh!*" The same woman frowned at Brian, so he whispered even more softly.

"It fell off the float. Nobody got hurt, but—"

"*Shhhh!*" the woman said. "You're inter-rupting the speeches."

"I'll tell you later," Brian said. Trying to be patient, he took a good look at the row of officials. Harry Harlow had finished his speech, and Councilman Williford was speaking about his grandfather.

Mayor Harlow didn't even pretend to lis-ten. He wiggled in his rickety folding chair and fidgeted nervously with the end of his tie. Emma Wegman, who had brought the largest handbag Brian had ever seen, seemed just as nervous. She clasped and unclasped her hands and crossed and uncrossed her ankles. Only Mr. Vlado, who hunched over, chuckling to himself, seemed to be having a good time.

As Mr. Williford came to the end of a long, boring sentence, the mayor interrupted. He jumped to his feet and grabbed the micro-phone. "Thank you, Councilman," he said.

"Now it's time to open the capsule."

Hugh Dickerson stepped down into the dirt around the capsule. Next to him was a man who looked so much like him, he had to be his brother Gene. The dirt had been loosened and shoveled back from the capsule, so it took only a minute for the two men to lift out the time capsule and place it upright in front of the mayor.

"Will you break the seal, please?" the mayor asked.

Hugh Dickerson pulled a screwdriver from his belt, poked it into the soft red wax that circled the top of the capsule, and pried the strip of wax loose.

As everyone leaned forward, the mayor pulled off the lid and peered into the container.

Suddenly he gasped and staggered back. The lid dropped to the ground. "It's empty!" Mayor Harlow shouted. "The time capsule is empty!"

# 5

ALTHOUGH EVERYONE began talking at once, the mayor could still be heard. He bellowed for the police chief. "Find the culprit! Catch the thief who did this!"

Brian and Sean looked at each other.

"The mayor looks scared," Sean said.

"Maybe he's a good actor," Brian suggested.

"How could he have taken the stuff from the capsule? How could anybody?" Sean asked. "You saw Mr. Dickerson peel the wax seal off."

"That's our first clue that someone opened the capsule and resealed it," Brian said. He pulled Sean away from the crowd so they could talk. "Remember when we were here before? We saw the wax that was put on the capsule back in 1918. It was hard and dried out. The wax Mr. Dickerson peeled off was soft. That means it was a new seal."

"But how could anybody open the capsule? The Dickerson brothers and the police took turns guarding it."

"How about when the space shuttle crashed?" Brian asked. "Everybody ran to see what had happened. The thief would have had ten or fifteen minutes to cut through the old wax, pull out the contents of the capsule, and slap the strip of fresh wax around the edge."

Sean gave a loud sigh of relief. "That means somebody wasn't trying to get rid of me." He looked to both sides before he added, "And the shuttle wasn't pushed over by Mr. Vlado's ghosts."

"Right," Brian said. "The thief wanted to cause a distraction."

Sean thought a moment. "Why did the thief

take everything in the capsule, and not just the newspaper?"

"If only the newspaper was missing, the police could look up the November issue, the way we did. Then Mayor Harlow would look guilty."

"He is guilty, isn't he?"

"We don't know. The thief might have been Miss Wegman. Or someone we haven't even thought of. We don't know what else was in that time capsule that could cause problems for someone." Brian sighed. "This is going to be a tough case to solve."

"Wait a minute," Sean said. "Dad told us the case was closed."

"That was the first case, where we were trying to find all the 1918 fourth graders," Brian said. "This is a different case. Now we have to find a thief."

Sean thought a minute, then nodded in agreement. "What do we do next?" he asked.

"We can't look for footprints. If the thief left footprints in the dirt around the capsule, they were wiped out by the Dickersons."

"Let's take a look at the site anyhow," Brian said. He led the way, edging through the people who were still milling about. Sean followed. "If I'm right about the fresh wax, we'll find small flecks of the old, dried wax in the dirt."

"Bingo!" Sean said as he bent over the hole. he pointed at a few small slivers of red. "Look over there . . . and there."

Brian pulled tweezers and a small plastic bag from the pocket of his jeans. He stepped into the hole and picked up a few pieces of the red wax.

"Hey, you! Get out of there!" Hugh Dickerson yelled.

Brian looked up. The Quinns' friend, Detective Thomas Kerry, had been talking to both Dickersons, and they looked very uncomfortable. Hugh's face and head were an angry red.

"You ought to chase those boys away!" he growled at Detective Kerry. "They've been snooping around here before. I wouldn't be surprised if they stole the stuff in the time capsule."

"Yikes!" Sean said. "We didn't do it!"

"But we would like to talk to you, Detective Kerry," Brian said. Brian stepped out of the hole and held up the plastic bag. "I'd like to tell you what I think about the wax seal."

Detective Kerry listened intently, but the Dickerson brothers glowered.

When Brian had finished his explanation, detective took the bag and said, "Thank y We'll check this out."

Mr. Vlado hobbled up and peered around Detective Kerry's shoulder.

"Are you going to check for fingerprints on the soft wax seal and on the capsule?" Sean asked the detective.

Brian answered before Detective Kerry could. "There won't be fingerprints. If the thief had any sense at all, he would have worn gloves."

Gene Dickerson gave a start. Hugh Dickerson glanced toward the toolshed.

"However, the red dye in the wax might leave stains on the gloves," Brian added thoughtfully.

"I don't know where my gloves are," Hugh Dickerson said. "I lost them."

"I threw my gloves away," Gene Dickerson said. "They had a hole in them."

Mr. Vlado chortled. "No you didn't," he said. "Your gloves are sticking out of your back pocket."

He whipped them out of Gene Dickerson's pocket and held them up. "Aha!" Mr. Vlado said. "Red stains!"

"The stains came from pulling the seal off the capsule," Gene Dickerson insisted. He turned to Detective Kerry. "You saw me take it off. Everybody saw me."

"Yeah!" Hugh Dickerson said. "Don't listen to anything those nosy kids tell you!"

"I'd check the toolshed," Brian told Detective Kerry. "Hugh Dickerson's gloves might be in the toolshed."

"And the contents of the time capsule," Mr. Vlado said. "We wouldn't want to lose those fourth-grade letters, would we?" He laughed so hard he nearly fell over.

Detective Kerry ignored the Dickerson brothers and spoke to Brian. "According to what I've been told, you were in this area earlier. Did you see anything else you think you should report? Anything out of the ordinary?"

Brian hesitated only a moment. "If we think of anything, we'll let you know."

Sean said, "We found a news—"

"A newspaper story that told all about the planners of the ceremony. We'll read it again and see if it gives us any other ideas."

"Brian! Sean!" Mrs. Quinn waved and called. "Hurry! We're leaving."

As they skirted the crowd to join their parents, Sean asked, "Bri, you didn't let me tell Detective Kerry about the 1918 newspaper article. Why not?"

"Because Mayor Harlow and Miss Wegman might not be the guilty ones. That newspaper article could make the police think they are, and they wouldn't investigate the Dickersons."

"Do you think Mr. Vlado was right about the stolen stuff being hidden in the toolshed?" Sean asked.

Brian glanced back over his shoulder. "I don't know. Hugh and Gene Dickerson were awfully nervous about being questioned. Since they were guards, they had a better chance than anyone at stealing the contents of the capsule."

"Why would they want to steal the stuff in the capsule? There wouldn't be anything about them in it."

Brian lowered his voice. "The thief didn't have to do the job himself. He could have hired somebody to steal for him."

"Should we look in the toolshed?"

"No," Brian said. "That would be illegal. It's up to Detective Kerry to get a search warrant if he wants to check out the toolshed."

"We need to make a list of suspects," Sean said. "So far we've got the Dickerson brothers, Emma Wegman, and Mayor Harlow."

"And maybe Councilman Williford," Brian said.

"Why him?" Sean asked.

"I'm guessing that he knows what the gift to the city is. Maybe it's something valuable. It could be something he wants for himself."

"He's standing right over there talking to some people. Why don't we ask him if he knows what the gift is?"

"Good idea, and then there's one more

thing we have to do."

"Brian, Sean, I told you to hurry," Mrs. Quinn said as she joined them.

"Sorry, Mom," Sean said.

"If it's okay with you and Dad, just go on without us," Brian said. "Sean and I have to make a trip to the library."

Mrs. Quinn smiled. "All right," she said. "Just be home by five. We're going to have an early dinner."

As soon as their parents had left, Brian and Sean ran to catch Mr. Williford, who was striding toward his car.

"Mr. Williford," Brian called, "could we please ask you one question?"

"If it doesn't take too long," Mr. Williford answered. He stood tall and elegant in a dark blue suit that looked as if it cost an awful lot of money. "What is your question?"

"We read about your grandfather in *California Pix* in the library," Sean said.

Mr. Williford's eyes widened in surprise. "That old issue? Surely they wouldn't have kept it in the library all these years?"

"It's on tape," Sean explained. "We had to read it in the microfilm machine."

"Your grandfather gave the city a gift," Brian said. "It was in the capsule. Do you know what the gift is? Did he ever tell you?"

"No, he didn't." Mr. Williford looked at his watch.

"That means the police don't know what they're looking for," Sean said.

"I'm afraid that's right. Now, please excuse me. I'm late for an appointment."

Still frowning, Mr. Williford hurried to his car and quickly drove out of the parking lot.

Sean sighed. "It would have helped a lot if he knew."

"I think he does," Brian said. "He didn't want to answer our question."

"He had to go. He was late for an appointment."

Brian shook his head. "He lied about having an appointment," he said. "The ceremonies would still be going on if the contents of the time capsule hadn't been stolen."

"That means Mr. Williford is one of our suspects."

"Let's go to the library," Brian said. "That photograph of Mr. Williford's grandfather has been bugging me. I want to take another look at it."

It was only a six-block walk, but as usual on a Saturday morning, the library was crowded, so Brian and Sean had to wait until one of the librarians could write down their request for the *California Pix* tape and go into the room where the tapes where kept to get it for them.

Brian glanced toward the far wall where the microfilm machines stood empty. "Good," he said. "Nobody's using the machines. We can thread a machine as soon as we get the tape."

But the wait was a long one, and when the librarian returned to the counter she was empty-handed.

"According to our records, you checked out the tape last," she said.

"We turned it in before we left," Brian told her. "That should be in your records, too."

"It is," she said. "And I clearly remember putting the tape back on the shelf in its proper place." She looked unhappy. "We have a problem," she told them. "The tape is missing."

# 6

BRIAN LAID SOME slices of cheese and lunch meat on a piece of bread and slapped another slice of bread on top. "Big mistake," he said. "We told Councilman Williford where the magazine article was and even how to find it."

Sean had his mouth open to bite into the sandwich he'd made for himself, but he stopped. "Do you think he stole the tape?"

"Who else?" Brian answered.

"Why would he do that? The article said only nice things about his grandfather."

"I know, but there was something else in that photo story. Something that might have been a clue."

Brian pulled out his notebook and pen and wrote, "Councilman Victor Williford." Underneath he wrote,

> (1) Does he know what his grand-father's missing "gift to the city" was? (2) He didn't want capsule to be opened. Why? (3) Did he take the tape of *California Pix* from the library? If he did, then why?

"LOTS OF QUESTIONS, NO ANSWERS," Sean said. He finished his sandwich and wiped his mouth on the back of his hand. "What are you going to write about Mayor Harry Harlow?"

"That he was eager to open the capsule right away. He wanted to be in charge of it and keep it in his office until the date of the ceremonies."

"Don't forget to write what was in the newspaper article."

"I won't. That's important," Brian said. He jotted down his notes about the mayor and went on to include suspect number three: Emma Wegman.

"She had just as much reason as the mayor to not want people to see that copy of the 1918 newspaper," Brian said.

"She was awfully nervous during the ceremony," Sean said. "Do you think it was because she knew the capsule had been opened?"

"I don't know," Brian said. "The mayor was nervous, too."

Sean giggled. "So were Hugh and Gene Dickerson, after their talk with Detective Kerry."

He watched Brian write, then asked, "Do you think the police searched the toolshed?"

"I hope so," Brian said.

"How long would it take to get a search warrant?"

Brian shrugged. "First, Detective Kerry would have to find a judge on duty. Then, he'd have to give him a good reason why he needed to have the toolshed searched."

"That could take hours," Sean said. "The Dickersons would have had time to get rid of their gloves and hide the stuff they took from the capsule."

Brian thought a moment. "We haven't talked about hiding the stuff. Let's see. . . . Mr. Williford could have hid it in the trunk of his car."

"So could the mayor, in *his* car."

"And Miss Wegman had that huge handbag. It could hold a lot."

"Everything that was in the time capsule?"

"Probably."

"All our suspects have motives," Sean said.

"And opportunity," Brian said. "I think it's time to have a talk with some of them. We know where Miss Wegman lives. Let's visit her first."

Sean looked around the kitchen. "We'd better clean up first, or Mom might have something to say about it."

It took just a few minutes for Brian and Sean to clean the kitchen and ride their bikes to Miss Wegman's house.

"Good," Sean said, as they rang the doorbell. "Debbie Jean's not hanging around. I didn't want to run into her."

But the moment Miss Wegman opened the door, Debbie Jean stepped up beside her. "Sean Quinn!" she said. "What are you doing here?"

Sean groaned, but Brian introduced himself and Sean to Miss Wegman. "We'd like to ask you some questions," he said.

"Sean and Brian are detectives," Debbie Jean told Miss Wegman. "They sometimes call on me to help them with their hardest cases."

Brian corrected her. "We're private investi-gators. May we please come in? Our ques-tions won't take long."

"Of course you may come in," Miss Wegman said, but as soon as they had all been seated in the living room she suddenly looked at them with suspicion. "Aren't you the boys who accused Hugh Dickerson of not doing his job?"

"Not exactly," Sean said.

But Brian looked stern. "He was away from his post," he said. "You saw what hap-pened when the capsule was opened." He took out his notebook and pen.

Miss Wegman sighed. "What a terrible morning. I was nervous to begin with, because I hate crowds. And the bag of items to place inside the new capsule was heavy. And I hated having everyone read again that newspaper story about my stupid, thieving cousin."

"You weren't trying to hide the story?"

Sean asked in surprise.

"Of course not. Everyone in Redoaks knew that Wegman and Harlow robbed the bank. You boys are too young to remember, but Mayor Harlow even used the story in his first campaign. He gave speeches about doing good for the community to make up for the bad his great-uncle had done."

"Do you know why he wanted to open the capsule early?"

"He wanted to settle that story, once and for all. It bothered him that future Redoaks citizens might tie him in with his great-uncle's illegal activities."

"Just two more questions," Brian said. "You found the file that told the contents of the time capsule, didn't you? Was there anything in that file about John Williford's gift to the city? Do you know what it was?"

Debbie Jean sniffed. "That was *three* questions."

"There was nothing in the file but the list of contents," Miss Wegman said. "I suppose the gift was Mr. Williford's secret. It wouldn't be made known until the capsule was opened." She paused. "I've wondered if Mr. Williford ever told his grandson anything about the gift. Maybe Councilman Williford knows what it is."

"He might," Brian said. "We're going to talk to him, too."

Miss Wegman frowned. "Maybe you shouldn't," she said. "Councilman Williford is used to getting his own way, and he doesn't like to be questioned. Between you and me, I think his grandfather spoiled him when he was young."

"I want to go with you," Debbie Jean said.

"You can't," Sean told her.

"We'll see about that," Debbie Jean insisted.

Brian closed his notebook and stood. Sean jumped up, too. "Thanks for your help, Miss Wegman," Brian said.

A few minutes later, as Brian and Sean climbed on their bikes, Brian said, "If we just knew what that gift to the city was, it would make our job a lot easier."

"Where are we going now?" Sean asked.

"To the park," Brian told him. "I want to talk to the Dickerson brothers."

When they arrived at the park some mothers and little kids were in the playground, but the area that had been crowded that morning was empty. Even the trash had been picked up.

As Sean glanced around nervously, he caught a flash of movement near the heavy trunk of one of the oak trees. "Brian," he whispered. "Somebody's hiding and spying on us. Do you think it's the Dickersons?"

Brian didn't even look back. "It's Debbie Jean," he said. "She followed us on her bike."

"She's going to ruin everything," Sean said.

"Forget Debbie Jean," Brian said. "We need to find the Dickerson brothers. I wonder if they're in the toolshed." He headed toward the shed, and Sean had to run to catch up.

"We're not going in there, are we?" Sean asked, his heart thumping as they neared the small, boxy building with its lone, small window on one side.

"I don't know," Brian said. "They might not let us in. They might not want to talk to us."

The door was shut, but the padlock was nowhere in sight. Wind whistled around the shed. The trees sighed and shivered. Sean shivered, too. "Let's get out of here!" he said.

But Brian reached up and knocked on the door.

No one answered.

He knocked again, more loudly.

Hinges creaking, the door slowly swung open.

# 7

N O ONE'S HERE," Brian said. He glanced around the room, which was empty of all but tools. "I don't see any gloves. And there's nothing here that could hold the contents of the time capsule."

He pulled the door shut. "We'll see if the Dickersons' addresses are in the phone book and visit them later."

"Are we going home now?" Sean asked. He still had the creepy feeling that the Dickersons were hiding somewhere and might pop out and chase them.

"Not yet," Brian said. "I've been thinking.

I read something about letters from important people being valuable," he said. "I wonder what that letter written by Governor William D. Stephens would be worth?"

"It's not like Governor Stephens was a movie star or a president or anything like that," Sean said. "Besides, how will we find out if the letter's worth anything at all?"

"A philatelist might know," Brian said.

"A *who*?"

"A philatelist," Brian said. "A postage stamp collector."

"Oh. Why didn't you just say so in the first place?" Sean said. "Jabez's grandfather owns a shop for stamp collectors. It's downtown on Main Street."

"He might be able to tell us about letters as well as stamps," Brian said. "Let's go talk to him."

Mr. Amadi's shop was small, but hundreds —maybe thousands—of postage stamps from around the world were displayed in glass cases. Sean wondered if the many drawers were also filled with stamps.

Debbie Jean sidled in the door, joining them at the counter.

"Go home," Sean said.

"No. I'm helping you," Debbie Jean told him.

They waited while Mr. Amadi sold a stamp to a customer. Sean began to forget about what a pest Debbie Jean was as he thought about how much fun it would be to collect stamps with kings and queens on them, or with horses, or . . .

"Hello, Sean. Hello, Debbie Jean," Mr. Amadi said. "What can I do for you?"

Sean introduced Brian, who said, "We want to know what a letter from a former governor might be worth."

Mr. Amadi shrugged. "I'm afraid I can't answer that question," he said. "There are collectors who specialize in letters and documents. I specialize in stamps. If you can tell me what stamp was on the letter, I could possibly answer your question. The stamp might, or might not, be worth something."

Brian felt discouraged. "I saw a photograph of the letter, but I didn't pay much attention to the stamp."

"Yes, you did," Sean said in surprise. "I said it was weird, and you agreed and asked me if I saw it, too."

"I was talking about the strange expression on old John Williford's face."

"Oh," Sean said. "I was talking about the stamp."

"What was weird about the stamp?" Mr. Amadi asked.

"The airplane on it," Sean said. "It was flying upside down."

Mr. Amadi gave such a start he dropped the pencil he'd been holding. "What year are you talking about?" he asked. "What year was the

SECRET OF THE TIME CAPSULE 71

letter mailed?"

"In 1918," Sean answered.

Mr. Amadi clutched the edge of the counter. "Oh, oh, oh!" he said. "If what I suspect is true, you have seen a photograph of a very rare and valuable stamp. In 1918, the United States government issued one hundred airmail stamps before anyone noticed they'd printed the picture of the airplane upside down."

"Would a stamp collector in 1918 have known the stamp was valuable?" Brian asked.

"A serious collector would know it was worth a great deal of money and that it would continue to grow in value," Mr. Amadi said.

"How valuable do you mean?" Brian asked.

"It's impossible to put a price tag on that stamp," Mr. Amadi explained. "I haven't seen any of them listed for sale in recent years. I do remember, though, that one of the upside-down airplane stamps sold at auction in 1979 for $135,000. And in 1989, a block of four sold for $1.1 million at an auction. I'm not sure exactly how much someone would pay today—maybe as much as $250,000."

Brian and Sean looked at each other. "The gift for the city," Sean said. "Now we know what it was!"

Brian frowned. "So does Councilman Williford."

Mr. Amadi seemed puzzled. "Councilman Victor Williford is one of my clients. He inherited his grandfather's excellent stamp collection and has continued it. Does he have the stamp?"

"We aren't sure," Brian answered, "but we're doing our best to find out."

# 8

B RIAN USED Mr. Amadi's phone to leave a message for Detective Kerry. In the message he told what he and Sean suspected and where they were going.

"This is a serious matter. Perhaps I should come with you," Mr. Amadi said.

"Me, too," Debbie Jean said.

Brian shook his head. "We've added up the facts, and Councilman Williford is our number one suspect," he said. "But we don't have the proof yet."

As Sean and Brian headed north on their bikes, Sean asked, "Councilman Williford's house is that big gray stone house on the hill. Right?"

"Right. And if Mr. Williford has the stamp, he won't have had a chance to sell it yet, so it will still be in his house," Brian said.

"I don't think he'll invite us in. He'll know we've come looking for that stamp," Sean said.

"We need an excuse to get inside," Brian said. "Is your school selling any spaghetti supper tickets or band candy?"

"Wrong time of the year," Sean said.

Brian grinned. "My school's having seventh-grade career day next month. I'll invite the councilman to be one of the speakers."

It was a short, uphill ride to the large house Councilman Williford had inherited from his grandfather, so within ten minutes Brian and Sean were on the doorstep, ringing the bell.

The maid, who answered the door, listened to Brian's explanation and let them in. "You'll have to sit there and wait a few minutes," she said, pointing to a carved, wooden bench. "Councilman Williford is entertaining some guests."

As soon as she had left, Brian whispered to Sean, "Remember that article in *California Pix*? It said that John Williford kept his stamps on display in a special room next to the entry hall. Come on. We'll have time to take a quick look."

Sean followed Brian to a carved wooden door. The handle turned easily, and the boys stepped into the room. Brian flipped the light switch and shut the door behind them.

Stamps were everywhere. Some were framed and hanging on the wall. Some were in display cases. And there were books of stamps on shelves. Sean opened the cover of the nearest one and saw rows of stamps, each protected by small plastic pockets.

He groaned. "There are too many stamps! How will we ever find the upside-down airplane stamp?"

"It probably isn't even in this room," Brian said. "I guess that he's hidden it somewhere else for now. Someplace very private, like his home office or his bedroom. Let's try his office."

As quietly as they could they left the entry hall. On the right was a large living room, and they could see a dining room beyond. On the left was a wide hallway and three closed doors.

Carefully, silently, Brian opened the first door. "This is it!" he whispered. He pulled Sean inside the room and turned on the light. Before them was a large U-shaped desk. On one end of the desk rested a computer and telephone.

"Look on the desk for the envelope," Brian said.

But Sean grabbed Brian's arm and pointed to a wastepaper basket. In it they could see an old, yellowed newspaper, a copy of *California Pix*, a stack of black-and-white photos of smiling faces, and a thick manila envelope. "That's gotta be the stuff from the time capsule!" Sean said. "The letter with the upside-down airplane stamp must be in this room!"

Sliding doors at one side of the room suddenly rolled open. Councilman Williford stood in the doorway, scowling at Brian and Sean.

"So you know about the stamp," he said, holding up the envelope Brian and Sean had seen in the magazine. "I had hoped you wouldn't notice it in the photo."

"It's not your stamp," Brian told him. "It belongs to the city."

"It belongs to me," the councilman snapped. "My grandfather was foolish to give it away."

Brian began edging backward, pulling Sean with him, but Councilman Williford said, "Stay where you are. You won't be leaving this house. I can't afford to let you go."

"There are two of us," Brian said. "And only one of you."

Councilman Williford smiled. "Then I'd

better bring in some of my friends—the friends who helped me obtain the stamp."

Hugh and Gene Dickerson squeezed into the doorway next to him. Brian gulped and Sean yelled, "Yikes!"

Brian and Sean hadn't heard the door to the hall open, but suddenly Debbie Jean spoke from behind them. "Brian and Sean brought some of their friends, too," she said.

"That's right," Miss Wegman said. "Mr. Amadi called me. He was worried about what the boys were up to by themselves, and I was, too."

Mr. Vlado hobbled forward. "We've got extra help," he said, and winked at Sean. "Some friends from the cemetery who don't like the way you tampered with their time capsule."

"And the police are on their way," Mr. Amadi added.

"So don't anybody move," Debbie Jean said. She beamed at Sean. "I always wanted to say that."

There were loud footsteps in the hall, orders from Detective Kerry, and soon the Dickersons and Councilman Williford were taken into custody.

"Let's have a party and celebrate!" Mr. Amadi said.

"Right now!" Miss Wegman glanced at the contents of the wastepaper basket. "We'll have a second opening of the time capsule."

Brian looked at his watch. "Not yet!" he said. "Mrs. Jackson should be on hand when the fourth graders' letters are opened. And as for Sean and me, we may have solved another case, but we're going to be in big trouble if we get home late for dinner!"

JOAN LOWERY NIXON is a renowned writer of children's mysteries. She is the author of more than eighty books and the only four-time recipient of the prestigious Edgar Allan Poe Award for the best juvenile mystery of the year.

☾

"*I was asked by* Disney Adventures *magazine if I could write a short mystery. I decided to write about two young boys who help their father, a private investigator, solve crimes. These boys, Brian and Sean, are actually based on my grandchildren, who are the same ages as the characters. My first Casebusters story was a piece about a ghost that haunts an inn. This derives from a legendary Louisiana inn I visited which was allegedly haunted. Later, I learned the owner had made up the entire tale, and I used that angle in the story.*"

— JOAN LOWERY NIXON

## *Secret of the Time Capsule*

Here's a secret code from the Casebusters! You can use it to write messages to your friends and to decode the Casebusters' Crimesolving Tip below.

### **Secret Code**

The first letter of the word is written on one line, the second letter on the line below it, and so on. For example *Casebusters* would be written as:

C S B S E S

\/\/\/\/

A E U T R

The top line is then connected to the bottom line with a hyphen to create the "word" CSBSES-AEUTER.

### **Secret Message**

CSBSES'-AEUTER CIEOVN-RMSLIG TP-I #-6 DTCIE-EETUS AWY-LAS KE-EP A NTPD-OEA HNY-AD T-O WIE-RT DW-ON DSRPIN-ECITOS O-F SSET-UPCS LCNE-IES PAE-LT NMES-UBR AD-N OHR-TE NTS-OE.